PINKY and REX
and the
New Neighbors

PINKY and REX
and the
New Neighbors

by James Howe
illustrated by Melissa Sweet

READY-TO-READ

ALADDIN PAPERBACKS

Aladdin Paperbacks
An imprint of Simon & Schuster Children's Publishing Division
1230 Avenue of the Americas
New York, New York 10020

READY-TO-READ is a registered trademark of Simon & Schuster, Inc.

Book design by Ethan Trask

The text of this book is set in Utopia.
The illustrations are rendered in watercolor.

First Aladdin Paperbacks Edition, 1997

Manufactured in the United States of America

10 9 8

The Library of Congress has cataloged the Atheneum Books for Young
Readers Edition as follows:

Howe, James, 1946–
Pinky and Rex and the new neighbors / by James Howe ; illustrated by
Melissa Sweet.—1st ed.
p.   cm.
Summary: Rex and her best friend Pinky are upset to learn that their friend
and neighbor Mrs. Morgan is moving, and it looks like a family with an
obnoxious boy named Ollie is set to move in.
ISBN-13: 978-0-689-80022-1   ISBN-10: 0-689-80022-3 (hc.)
ISBN-13: 978-0-689-81296-5   ISBN-10: 0-689-81296-5 (pbk.)
[1. Moving, Household—Fiction. 2. Neighborliness—Fiction. 3. Friendship—
Fiction.] I. Sweet, Melissa, ill. II. Title.
PZ7.H83727Pim   1997
[Fic]—dc20
95-42543
CIP   AC

In memory of Aunt Bea
—J. H.

To my neighbors, Debbie & Sara
—M. S.

to
Hunter.
Melissa Sweet
2008

Contents

Chapter 1
Bad News

The first Rex heard about it was from her babysitter. Mara was putting fingernail polish on Rex at the time, something Rex allowed only Mara to do because she used cool colors like green and purple. At the moment, Mara was painting Rex's nails blue with sparkles.

"Good news about Mrs. Morgan,

isn't it?" Mara said, referring to Rex's neighbor.

"What news?" Rex asked.

"Haven't you heard?" Mara seemed surprised. "She's moving. Now maybe you'll have somebody *nice* living next door."

Without thinking, Rex twisted her body away to look in the direction of Mrs. Morgan's house.

"Careful!" Mara said.

"Sorry," said Rex, giving her hand back to the babysitter. "I just . . . I didn't know Mrs. Morgan was moving."

Mara studied Rex's face. "Aren't you glad? You look almost sad or something."

Rex shrugged. "I am, sort of."

"But why? She's a mean old witch, remember?"

Rex remembered that a "mean old witch" was what all the kids in the neighborhood had once called Mrs. Morgan. It wasn't a nice name, but it fit her. She *had* been mean, but then she changed. She'd become a special friend to Rex and her best friend Pinky. She gave them cookies and lemonade on hot days, cookies and cocoa on cold ones. She had shown them faded photographs of herself when she was their age and given each of them a book from her childhood with her name printed inside the front cover in pencil.

"She's not so bad," Rex said at last.

Mara, who had been Rex's babysitter since she was little, shook her head. "That's not what you used to say."

"I know. But I like her now."

Mara put the last drop of polish on Rex's nails and closed the bottle. "So I guess it isn't good news," she said.

"No," said Rex. She just couldn't imagine the house next door without Mrs. Morgan in it.

Chapter 2
For Sale

Pinky couldn't imagine it either.

"I thought she'd always be there," he said to Rex as they played in Rex's backyard.

"Me, too," said Rex. "Did you see the sign?"

Pinky nodded. A FOR SALE sign had gone up in front of Mrs. Morgan's house that morning.

"I wonder who's going to move in," Rex went on.

"Maybe they'll have kids," Pinky said. Suddenly he was worried. "We'll still be best friends, right?"

"Of course."

"Even if a girl moves in next door?"

Rex gave Pinky a look. "Don't be

dumb," she said.

Pinky smiled.

Mrs. Morgan shouted hello from her backyard. Pinky and Rex went running. Minutes later, they were helping her set up her easel. "I never realized there were so many things in this yard I wanted to paint," Mrs. Morgan said. "And now I have so little time to do it."

"You could come back to visit," said Rex.

Mrs. Morgan smiled sweetly at her young friend. "I don't think the new people would care to have me roaming around their yard with my paints and easel," she said.

"Who *are* the new people?" Pinky asked.

"I have no idea," Mrs. Morgan

replied. "No one has even looked at the house yet. But someone *will* buy it. And then it will be theirs. Oh, my," she said with a sudden faraway look in her eyes. "It won't be mine anymore. After thirty-seven years. Imagine that."

"Why do you have to move?" Pinky asked.

"I don't," she answered. "But I want to. Now don't take that the wrong way. I'm not tired of my neighbors. It's just that when you get to be my age it becomes harder to take care of a house. And even though I enjoy your company, I don't have many other visitors. I get lonely."

"Are you moving far away?" asked Rex, watching as Mrs. Morgan began to squeeze some color from a tube onto her wooden palette.

"I'm moving into a housing complex for seniors," she said, winking at the kids. "That means old folks like me. It's right here in town. I'll have my own apartment, so I can still bake cookies for you when you come to visit."

Rex broke into a big smile. "Neat!" she cried.

As Mrs. Morgan studied the flowers in her garden, deciding where to begin, she said, "I hope you'll visit often." She poked her brush into a dab of bright yellow and began to paint.

Chapter 3
Ollie

For days, Pinky and Rex kept an eye out for the man in the van. He was the one selling Mrs. Morgan's house. When his big gray van pulled up to the curb in front, they hid behind the bush in Rex's yard to see who would get out. So far, there had been an older couple with no children, a young couple with two children, a woman with a teenager, and a man with a briefcase. And then one day Ollie and his parents came.

Ollie was seven. He spotted the two children behind the bush at once. While his parents looked at the house, Ollie stayed outside and told Pinky and Rex all about himself. He had a cat named Sphinx and a dog named Charlene. His father was a pilot and his mother wrote television commercials. He had been riding a two-wheeler without training wheels since he was four. He had been reading since he was three. He could beat his father at chess. He was allowed to see any movie he wanted. He bet he got a bigger allowance than they did. He—

He was interrupted when his

mother called out, "Ollie, come and look at the room that will be yours!"

As the boy disappeared into Mrs. Morgan's house, Rex looked at Pinky in horror. "*He's* going to be my new neighbor?"

"He's the most obnoxious kid I

ever met," Pinky said. Then, feeling bad, he added, "But maybe he'll get better once we get to know him."

Mrs. Morgan's upstairs window must have been open. Either that, or Ollie had a very loud voice. Pinky and Rex heard him scream, "I *hate* this room! Why can't I have the big room? You *never* let me have what I want! If I can't have the big room, I'm not moving!"

"Or maybe he'll get worse," Rex said.

Pinky and Rex looked at each other. They couldn't believe this was happening.

Chapter 4

A Teddy Bear and a Trophy

"Not fair!" Pinky's little sister Amanda said for the fifth time that morning. Pinky ignored her as he headed toward the front door. Amanda followed fast on his heels.

"Well, it *isn't* fair that a big kid is moving in!" she went on. "You already have Rex to play with. I don't have anybody!"

Pinky turned around so fast Amanda bumped into him. "We'll let you play with Ollie, okay?" he said.

"But he's a boy! And he's seven!" Amanda protested.

Pinky shrugged. "I'm just trying to be fair," he said.

"Right," said Amanda. "You already told me you and Rex don't want to play with him. So why should I?"

Pinky shrugged again as he pushed open the door. "That's life," he called back over his shoulder.

Amanda stood fuming, her hand holding the screen door wide open. "Well, life's not fair!" she shouted after Pinky.

"Close the door!" her father called from inside the house.

"Not fair!" Pinky heard Amanda cry again as the door slammed shut.

Pinky chuckled to himself as he crossed the street. But then he thought,

It really isn't fair. He and Rex were best friends. They did everything together. Now there was going to be a boy their age who would live right next door to Rex, a boy they didn't even like. He'd want to play with them and they would have to let him. Things would never be the same.

Pinky found Rex in Mrs. Morgan's house. Boxes were everywhere.

"I'm helping Mrs. Morgan pack," Rex explained.

"I had no idea I had so much stuff," Mrs. Morgan said, coming in from another room. "Thank goodness the movers will be here tomorrow to pack most of it.

"Oh," she said, suddenly remembering the old teddy bear she

was holding. "This is William. He was mine as a child. Isn't it funny, Pinky, his name is the same as yours. Your *real* name, I mean. I'd like you to have him." She thrust the bear into Pinky's hands.

"Thank you," Pinky said, surprised. "I . . . I'll take good care of him."

"I know you will," Mrs. Morgan said. "That's why I'm giving him to you." Turning to Rex, she said, "There's something in the cellar I'd like you to have. It's too heavy for me to carry."

Exchanging curious looks, Pinky and Rex followed Mrs. Morgan down the narrow stairs.

"It's a trophy my father won," she explained to Rex. "I know you like sports, so I thought perhaps you'd want

it. My poor father didn't have any sons and I never had the least interest in sports. And of course my husband and I never had children . . . " Her voice trailed off.

"So," she asked Rex softly, "would you like it?"

"Oh, yes!" Rex said. "It's the biggest trophy I ever saw! Thanks, Mrs. Morgan."

"You're very welcome."

After they had carried the trophy upstairs, Mrs. Morgan invited them to join her for cookies. She apologized that they were store-bought, but explained that she hadn't had the time to bake. "You'll just have to visit me," she said.

As he took a bite of his cookie,

Pinky thought that Mrs. Morgan had
said they must come visit her as many
times that morning as Amanda had
said, "Not fair!"

   "At least," Mrs. Morgan said as she
opened the refrigerator to get some

milk, "you'll have nice new neighbors. I'm so happy the house was sold to such a lovely family."

Pinky and Rex looked at each other and rolled their eyes.

Chapter 5

The Empty House

"Do you remember the time we almost put Goopey-Goo in Mrs. Morgan's mailbox?" Rex asked Pinky.

Pinky nodded. "I'm glad we didn't do it," he said.

"Me, too," said Rex. The two friends were sitting on the front steps of the empty house next door. Mrs.

Morgan had been gone for two days.

"If we had," Rex went on, "she wouldn't have been our friend."

Pinky nodded again. "I'm glad she was," he said.

"Me, too," said Rex. "My dad says he'll take us to visit her on the weekend. He says the new neighbors are moving in on Saturday."

"And then we'll be stuck with O. O. forever," said Pinky. "I wish this house could just stay empty."

"What is O. O.?" Rex asked.

"Obnoxious Ollie," said Pinky.

Rex laughed. But it wasn't really funny.

Chapter 6
Mrs. Morgan's New Home

On Saturday morning, Pinky and Rex visited Mrs. Morgan.

"It's not really that far," Rex's father announced as they were settling into chairs in the tiny living room of her apartment. "Maybe next year the kids can ride their bikes here by themselves."

"Why can't we now?" Rex asked.

"A few too many busy streets to cross," he explained.

"I hope you'll still want to visit me next year," Mrs. Morgan said.

"We will," Pinky assured her. He sniffed the air and licked his lips.

"Peanut-butter cookies," Mrs. Morgan told him, as she crossed to the

kitchen. "So, what do you think of my new home?"

"It's nice," said Rex. Noticing that Mrs. Morgan had put some of her own paintings on the walls, she added, "You brought your backyard with you."

"Yes," Mrs. Morgan said, appearing with a plate of cookies. "And the best

part is that I can admire it without having to pull a single weed!"

Rex's father laughed at that. "By the way," he said, accepting a cookie, "we've invited the new neighbors for dinner tomorrow. Would you like to join us?"

"That's very nice of you," Mrs. Morgan said. "They're such lovely people. But I already have plans. My new neighbor is having a dinner party for me."

Soon it was time to say goodbye. "We promise to come back soon," Rex told Mrs. Morgan.

"Oh, I almost forgot," Pinky said. "William said to say hello."

Mrs. Morgan smiled. "Thank you," she said to Pinky. "It's always good to hear from an old friend."

Chapter 7
Friends

As they were driving home, Rex said to her father, "I don't understand why Mrs. Morgan keeps calling the new neighbors lovely. I guess she didn't get to know Ollie."

"Ollie?" her father said. "Who's Ollie?"

"Their son," said Rex. "He's obnoxious."

"Rex, that's not a nice thing to say about someone you don't even know. But I'm a little confused." He turned onto their street. "Oh, look," he said.

"There's the moving van. Our new neighbors are here."

Rex turned to Pinky. "Well," she said, "I guess we're going to have to play with O. O., whether we like it or not."

But when her father's car pulled into their driveway, Rex was in for a surprise. "It's not them," she said.

Amanda was running to the car, pulling a girl by the hand. "Ha, ha!" she cried. "You tricked me. There's no boy named Ollie. This is Samantha."

"Call me Sammi," the girl said.

"And she's *my* age!" Amanda said triumphantly. "We're going to be best friends!"

"No, we're not," said Sammi. "We're going to be sisters!"

Amanda hugged Sammi. "We're

going to be *best* sisters!" she said.

"I have a brother, too," Sammi informed Pinky and Rex as she ran off to Rex's backyard to play on the swings with her new best sister.

"Gee," said Rex, "I guess Ollie's

parents didn't buy the house, after all."

"I guess not," Pinky said. "But I wonder what Sammi's brother will be like." He noticed a woman walking towards them. She was holding a baby.

"I'm Sondra Leigh-Williams," she

said. "You must be Rex. And you're Pinky. I've been hearing all about both of you."

"Not from Amanda, I hope," said Pinky.

Mrs. Leigh-Williams smiled. "A little from Amanda, but mostly from Rex's mom. I found out you have a little brother almost the same age as my Michael. I understand you're wonderful with babies, Rex. Maybe you'll babysit for us when you're older."

"Me?" Rex laughed to think she'd ever be old enough to babysit.

Just then, Amanda and Sammi ran past. "We're going to my house to play dress-up!" Amanda shouted.

"I think those two are going to be great friends," Mrs. Leigh-Williams

said. "Wouldn't it be nice if Matthew and Michael became friends too?"

Rex nodded.

That night as she was lying in bed, she got to thinking how well everything had turned out. Mrs. Morgan had new friends, and so did Amanda and Matthew. She and Pinky could go on being best friends, just like always, now that they didn't have to worry about Ollie anymore. She hoped that wherever Ollie moved, he found a friend too, maybe someone who could help him not be so obnoxious.

Then, looking up at the trophy on the top of her dresser, she remembered the piece of paper she'd found folded inside.

It read: "Special Award to Rex. Best Next-Door Neighbor."

Smiling, Rex looked at the trophy for a long time. It was bright and shiny in the moonlight. When her eyes grew tired, she closed them and began thinking about babysitting for Sammi and Michael.

Moments later, she fell asleep. The smile was still on her face.